SKARLOEY

Based on *The Railway Series* by the Rev. W. Awdry

Illustrations by
Robin Davies and Phil Jacobs

TED SMART

Produced 2005 in Great Britain for The Book People Ltd,
Hall Wood Avenue, Haydock, St. Helens WA11 9UL
by Egmont Books Limited,
239 Kensington High Street,
London W8 6SA.

Thomas the Tank Engine & Friends

A BRITT ALLCROFT COMPANY PRODUCTION

Based on The Railway Series by The Rev W Awdry

ISBN 1 4052 0700 0
3 5 7 9 10 8 6 4 2
Printed in China

TO THE TRAINS ➡

This is a story about Skarloey the Narrow-Gauge Engine. Skarloey first came to my railway 100 years ago. Read about the troubles he had when he was brand new – and couldn't stop bouncing up and down!

Skarloey worked on the Little Railway, on the Island of Sodor.

He was 100 years old, but he was still a Useful Engine. All the other engines liked Skarloey and he would tell them stories about when he was young.

Everyone's favourite story was about the time Skarloey first came to the Little Railway.

Skarloey was built at the same time as another engine called Rheneas. They were both red, with four wheels each.

"We look wonderful," said Skarloey, proudly.

"We will pull coaches and everyone will want to ride in them!" replied Rheneas.

Skarloey and Rheneas were both going to work on the mountain line of the Little Railway. But Skarloey was finished first, so he had to go to the Little Railway alone, leaving Rheneas behind. The two engines felt sad when they said goodbye to each other.

Skarloey was sent away on a ship. It was very wobbly!

At the port they used the ship's cranes to lift Skarloey on to the shore. The ship's cranes were called 'derricks', and they nearly turned Skarloey upside down.

"How dare they treat me like this!" said Skarloey, crossly.

He was left hanging from the derricks for a long time. At last an engine arrived to take him to the mountain line.

"About time!" huffed Skarloey.

It was dark when Skarloey arrived at the mountain line. He felt lonely and miserable. "I wish Rheneas was here," he said, sadly.

Next morning there were trucks everywhere. They rattled and roared past Skarloey.

"There's no engine pulling them!" said Skarloey in surprise.

"The trucks come down the mountain by gravity," explained the Manager. "But the empty ones need taking up again. That's why you've come."

"What?" said Skarloey, crossly. "I don't want to pull trucks! Can't I pull coaches, Sir?"

"Certainly not," said the Manager. "We have to finish building this line, and for that, we need trucks. The Inspector is coming to look at the line soon."

Skarloey was furious. When the workmen tried to start him, his fire wouldn't burn. He made no steam – he just blew smoke at them. They tried again the next day, and the next, and the next. But Skarloey wouldn't do a thing!

Finally, the Manager lost his temper. "We're not going to look at your sulky face all day, Skarloey," he said. "We'll leave you alone until you're a better engine."

They covered Skarloey with a big sheet of tarpaulin and went away. Skarloey felt even more lonely and unhappy. Nobody talked to him.

At last the Manager came back. "I hope that you will be a better engine from now on," he said.

"Yes Sir, I will Sir!" said Skarloey, earnestly.

From then on, Skarloey worked very hard, and although he sometimes got too excited and would bounce up and down, the Manager was very pleased with his efforts.

By the time Rheneas arrived at last, the line was ready. Skarloey was delighted to see his old friend!

Rheneas soon settled in. One day, while he was shunting trucks, Skarloey hurried up to him. "I'm going to pull the Inspector's train, today!" said Skarloey.

"Be careful not to bounce," said Rheneas. "The Inspector won't like that."

But Skarloey was so excited, he just couldn't stop bouncing!

Skarloey had to take the Inspector up to the top of the mountain, and then back down again.

The upward journey went well and Skarloey felt very happy.

When it was time to go down, Skarloey was really excited. As they went faster and faster, he began to bounce! The coaches were scared. "He's playing tricks!" they said. "Bump him! Bump him!"

Just then, Skarloey gave an extra big bounce, and the Inspector lost his footing. He flew into a bush on the side of the line!

The Driver stopped the train. The Inspector was not hurt, but he was very cross!

"From now on, you will stay in the shed!" he said to Skarloey. "You are a bad engine!"

When the Inspector told the Manager what had happened, the Manager felt sorry for Skarloey. He knew that he had been trying very hard to be good.

"What Skarloey needs is an extra pair of wheels," he said. "Then he won't bounce any more." So Skarloey was sent off to the Works.

When Skarloey came back, Rheneas hardly recognised him. He had six wheels and a brand new cab, and he looked very smart.

"Now let's see what you can do," said the Manager. Sure enough, Skarloey found it much easier to travel along smoothly, without bouncing.

From then on, Skarloey pulled coaches and trucks up and down the track as easily as anything, and he didn't bounce his passengers once! And 100 years later, he is still as good as new!

The Thomas Story Library is THE definitive collection of stories about Thomas and ALL his Friends.

5 more Thomas Story Library titles will be chuffing into your local bookshop in April 2006:

´Arry and Bert
George
Jack
Annie and Clarabel
Rheneas

And there are even more
Thomas Story Library books to follow later!
So go on, start your Thomas Story Library NOW!

A Fantastic Offer for Thomas the Tank Engine Fans!

STICK
POUND
COIN
HERE

In every Thomas Story Library book like this one, you will find a special token. Collect 6 Thomas tokens and we will send you a brilliant Thomas poster, and a double-sided bedroom door hanger!

Simply tape a £1 coin in the space above, and fill out the form overleaf.

TO BE COMPLETED BY AN ADULT

To apply for this great offer, ask an adult to complete the coupon below and send it with a pound coin and 6 tokens, to:
THOMAS OFFERS, PO BOX 715, HORSHAM RH12 5WG

☐ Please send a Thomas poster and door hanger. I enclose 6 tokens plus a £1 coin. (Price includes P&P)

Fan's name...

Address...

....Postcode...........................

Date of birth..

Name of parent/guardian...

Signature of parent/guardian..

Please allow 28 days for delivery. Offer is only available while stocks last. We reserve the right to change the terms of this offer at any time and we offer a 14 day money back guarantee. This does not affect your statutory rights.

☐ Data Protection Act: If you do not wish to receive other similar offers from us or companies we recommend, please tick this box. Offers apply to UK only.